KT-161-860

Copyright © 1989 Brimax Books Ltd.
All rights reserved.
These stories have appeared as individual books.
This edition published by Brimax Books, Newmarket, England
First edition 1989
ISBN 0 86112 672 6
Printed in Portugal

Classic
Children's
Stories

ADAPTED BY LUCY KINCAID

ILLUSTRATED BY ERIC KINCAID

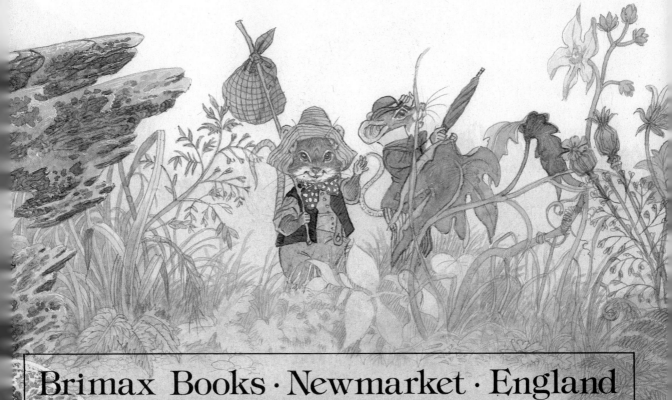

Brimax Books · Newmarket · England

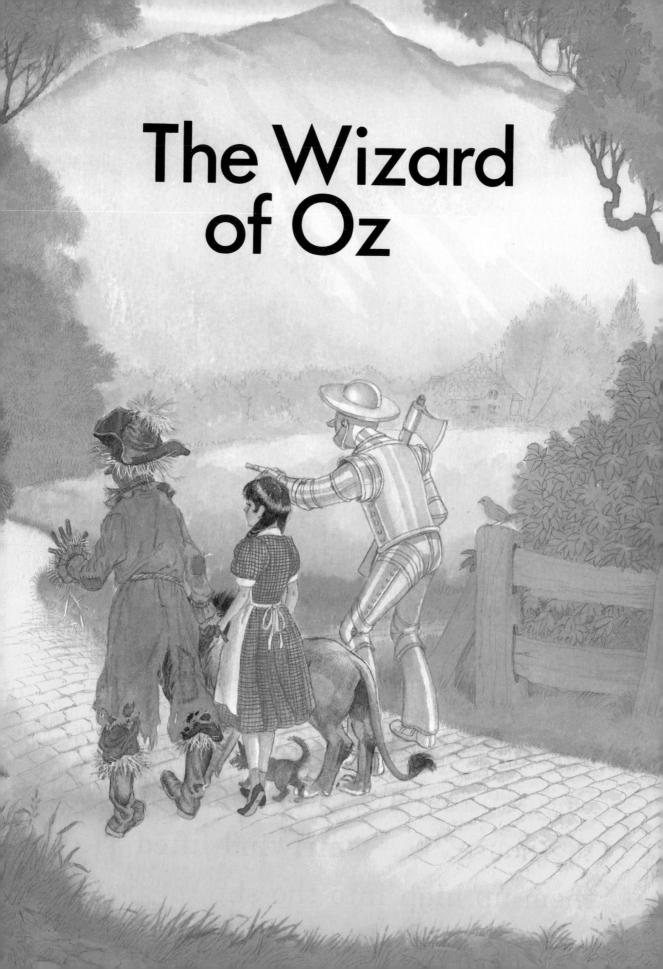

The Wizard of Oz

Dorothy lived with her Aunt Em
and Uncle Henry. She had a small
dog called Toto.
One day there was a whirlwind.
Dorothy and Toto were alone in
the house. The whirlwind lifted
them up high into the sky.

The house came to rest in the
Land of the Munchkins. It fell
on top of the Wicked Witch of
the East and killed her.
The Munchkins were very pleased.
They gave Dorothy the Wicked
Witch of the East's magic shoes.

"Can you help me find my way home?" she asked the Munchkins. They shook their heads. They did not know the way.

"Go to the Emerald City," they said. "Ask the Wizard of Oz to help you." Dorothy put on the magic shoes and set off along the yellow brick road with Toto.

After many miles
Dorothy met
a Scarecrow.
"Can I go to the
Emerald City with
you?" said the
Scarecrow. "Perhaps
the Wizard of Oz
will give me
a brain."

The next day they
found a Tin Man
in the forest.
"Can I go with
you?" said the Tin
Man. "Perhaps the
Wizard of Oz will
give me a heart."

A Lion jumped out of the bushes
and roared. It tried to bite Toto.
Dorothy slapped the Lion.
"How dare you bite a little dog!
You are a coward!" said Dorothy.
"I know," said the Lion. "But how
can I help it? Do you think the
Wizard of Oz would give me some
courage?"

They went across ditches and over rivers. At last they came to the Land of Oz. They went to the Emerald City. Everything in the city was green.

The Wizard of Oz lived in a palace. He was a magician. He could change the way he looked.

In the Throne Room all Dorothy
could see was a huge green head.
"I am Oz," said a voice. "Who
are you and why do you seek me?"
Dorothy told him she wanted
to find the way home.
"I will help if you kill the
Wicked Witch of the West," said
the Wizard.

The Scarecrow saw
the Wizard as
a green lady.

The Tin Man saw
the Wizard as
a wild animal.

The Lion saw him
as a ball of fire.

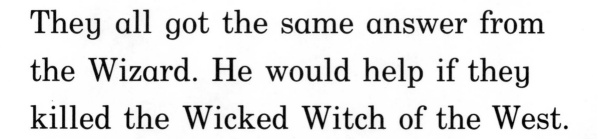

They all got the same answer from
the Wizard. He would help if they
killed the Wicked Witch of the West.

The Wicked Witch of the West
saw them coming. She tried to stop
them.

The Tin Man killed the wolves.
The Scarecrow caught the crows.
The bees broke their stings when
they tried to sting the Tin Man.
The Winkies ran away when the
Lion roared.

The Wicked Witch of the West was
angry. She sent the fierce Flying
Monkeys after them. They dropped
the Tin Man on to some rocks.
He broke into pieces. They pulled
the straw out of the Scarecrow.
They put the Lion into a cage.

The Flying Monkeys took Dorothy and Toto to the Wicked Witch's castle. The Witch saw Dorothy's magic shoes and began to shake. The Wicked Witch kicked Toto. That made Dorothy very angry.

She picked up a bucket of water
and threw it over the Witch.
Then as Dorothy looked on in
wonder, the Witch began to shrink
and fall away. Then there was
nothing but a puddle. The Wicked
Witch of the West was dead.

Dorothy let the Lion out of the cage. The Winkies helped her put the straw back into the Scarecrow. They helped her put the Tin Man back together.

When they returned to the palace
the Throne Room was empty. The
Lion gave a roar and knocked over
a screen. Hiding behind it was
a little man. It was the Wizard.
"I am not really a wizard," he said.
"People only think I am because I
can do tricks. But I will help you
if I can."

The Wizard filled
the Scarecrow's
head with sharp
things like pins
and needles.
"Now you have
a brain," he said.

He took a red silk
heart stuffed with
sawdust and put it
inside the Tin Man.

He gave the Lion
a drink that would
give him courage.

He made a balloon so that Dorothy
and Toto could fly home. The
balloon took off before Dorothy was
ready. It flew away without her.

The Good Witch of the South came
to rescue Dorothy.

"Tap your heels together three
times and tell the magic shoes
where you want to go," she said.

The Good Witch of the South made
the Scarecrow ruler of the Emerald
City. She made the Tin Man ruler
of the Winkies. She made the Lion
King of the Forest.
Dorothy and Toto went home
to Aunt Em and Uncle Henry.

All these appear in the pages of the story. Can you find them?

Dorothy and Toto

Scarecrow

Tin Man

Wicked Witch

Lion

Wizard

bucket

balloon

Use the pictures to tell the story
in your own words, and then draw
your own pictures.

Pinocchio

Old Geppetto was making a puppet.

As he cut the wood he heard a voice.

"Please do not hurt me," it said.

Geppetto looked all around.

He could not see anyone so

he went on with his work.

When he made the puppet's eyes,
they moved. When he made the mouth,
it laughed. When he made the feet,
they kicked.

"You are just like a real boy,"
said Geppetto.

He called the puppet Pinocchio.

Geppetto showed
Pinocchio how
to walk.

Naughty Pinocchio ran into the
street. Geppetto ran after him.
A policeman thought Geppetto was
being unkind. He took Geppetto
to the police station.

Pinocchio went home. He was very
pleased with himself.
"Boys who run away are sorry
in the end," said a talking
cricket. Pinocchio threw a hammer
at the cricket.
"I am taking no notice of you,"
he said.

Pinocchio went out
in the rain to
find some food.
Nobody would give
him any. He went
home hungry. He sat
by the fire and
fell asleep.

Geppetto knocked at
the door. Pinocchio
got up to answer it.
He fell to the floor.
"The fire has eaten
my feet," he cried.

Geppetto climbed
in through the
window.
"Don't worry,
Pinocchio," said
Geppetto. "I will
make you some
new feet. First
we shall have
something to eat."

Pinocchio was very pleased with
his new feet.
"I shall go to school and make you
proud of me," he said to Geppetto.
"But I need a reading book."
Geppetto sold his coat to buy
the reading book.

On his way to school Pinocchio saw a puppet theatre. He sold his book and paid to go in. He forgot all about school. He stayed all day and all night.

The puppet man gave him five gold coins to take home.

On the way home Pinocchio met a fox and a cat. The fox pretended to be lame. The cat pretended to be blind. They tried to trick Pinocchio out of his gold coins. Pinocchio ran away from them.

The fox and the
cat chased him.
They caught him
and tied him
to a tree.

He was rescued
by a fairy. She
took him home.
"How did this
happen?" she asked.

Pinocchio started to tell her the truth but he said he had lost the five gold coins. They were not lost. They were in his pocket. His nose began to grow.

His nose grew because he was telling lies.

His nose grew
very long indeed.
He could not
get it through
the door.
At last the fairy took pity on him.
She called some woodpeckers. The
woodpeckers pecked his nose back
to the right size.

Pinocchio wanted to see Geppetto.
"I shall go home now," said
Pinocchio. On the way he met
the fox and the cat. This time they
stole his money. Pinocchio told
a policeman. The policeman did not
believe him. He put Pinocchio
in prison.

A long time later Pinocchio came out
of prison. He went looking for
Geppetto again. Geppetto was
looking for Pinocchio. He went
to sea in a boat.

Pinocchio went to the seashore.
He saw Geppetto's boat tossed on
the waves. He swam out to help him.

Pinocchio met a dolphin in the sea.
"Geppetto has been swallowed by
a sea monster," said the dolphin.
Pinocchio sadly swam on. He
reached an island and met the fairy.
"I don't want to be a puppet," said
Pinocchio. "I want to be a boy."
"You can be a boy if you are good,"
said the fairy. "First you must
go to school."

Pinocchio tried to be good but
it was too hard. He ran away
to Toyland with some other naughty
boys. In Toyland they were all
so lazy they soon turned into
donkeys. Pinocchio was sold
to a circus. In the circus ring
Pinocchio fell and hurt his leg.

He was thrown into
the sea to drown.
But he turned back
into a puppet.
A sea monster
swallowed him.

What a surprise!
There inside the
fish Pinocchio
found Geppetto.
They hugged
each other.

"We can escape when the monster is asleep," said Pinocchio. They swam out of the monster's mouth. From that day on Pinocchio looked after Geppetto. Finally the fairy granted his wish. She made him into a real boy.

All these appear in the pages of the story. Can you find them?

Geppetto

Pinocchio

fox

cat

fairy

dolphin

donkeys

sea monster

Use the pictures to tell the story in your own words and then draw your own pictures.

The Snow Queen

Once there was a boy called Kay and a girl called Gerda. They were friends. They played together.

One winter's day, Kay's grandmother told them about the Snow Queen. "The Snow Queen brings the snow and ice," she said.

Kay thought he could see the
Snow Queen's face at the window.
She seemed to be calling to him.
He was afraid. He did not go.

The next day Kay went out with
his sledge. He saw a bigger
sledge. He tied his sledge to it
for a ride.

The big sledge set off. It went
faster and faster and far away.
When the sledge stopped, Kay saw
who was driving it. It was the
Snow Queen.

The Snow Queen
kissed Kay.
"My kiss will put
ice in your
heart," she said.

"You will forget
your home.
You will forget
Gerda."
She took Kay
to her palace.

Gerda wept when she could not find
Kay. She went to the river.
"I will give you my new red shoes,"
she said to the river. "Please
tell me where Kay is."
The river said nothing.

Gerda stepped into a boat. The
boat began to move. The river was
moving the boat.

An old woman
pulled in the boat.
She cast a spell
on Gerda to make
her forget Kay.

But one day Gerda
saw a painted rose.
It made her think
of him.
"I must find Kay,"
she said and off
she ran.

Gerda met a raven.
She told the raven
her story. The
raven knew of
a prince.
"Perhaps he is
Kay," said the
raven.
The raven took
Gerda to the
palace to see the
prince. But the
prince was not
Kay.
Gerda left
the castle in
a coach.

Robbers attacked the coach.
Gerda's life was saved by a little
robber girl. Gerda told the robber
girl she was looking for Kay.
The robber girl said, "I will help
you if I can."

That night a bird said to Gerda,
"I have seen Kay. He was with the
Snow Queen."
"Where were they going?" asked
Gerda.
"To the Land of Snow and Ice,"
said the bird.

"I come from that land," said
a reindeer. It belonged to the
robber girl. "I can take you
there," it said.
The robber girl agreed to set the
reindeer free.
"Take Gerda to find Kay," she said.

After many days
they came to the
Land of Snow and
Ice. They went
to see a wise
old woman.

She told the
reindeer, "You
must leave Gerda
at the Snow Queen's
garden."
The reindeer did
this.

Gerda was alone. The Snow Queen's guards tried to frighten her away. Little angels came to keep her safe.

65

Gerda went into
the palace. The
Snow Queen was
away. Kay was all
alone. Gerda ran
to greet him.

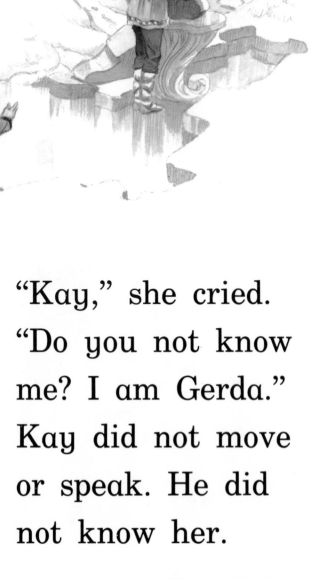

"Kay," she cried.
"Do you not know
me? I am Gerda."
Kay did not move
or speak. He did
not know her.

Gerda cried. Her hot tears fell
all over Kay. They melted the ice
in his heart. Now he knew who
Gerda was. Then Kay cried too.

"We must run away from here,"
said Kay. They ran to the garden.
The reindeer was waiting.

The reindeer carried them away.
They were safe from the Snow Queen
and they lived happily ever after.

All these appear in the pages of
the story. Can you find them?

Kay

Gerda

Snow Queen

sledge

rose

raven

prince

reindeer

Use the pictures to tell the story in your own words, and then draw your own pictures.

TOWN MOUSE!

Town Mouse
and Country Mouse

The second mouse lived in the
country. His house was on the edge
of a field. He was called the
country mouse.

The town mouse and the country
mouse met one day at a wedding.
They soon became friends.

One day the
country mouse sent
a letter to the
town mouse.
It said, "Would
you like to come
and stay with me
in the country?"

The town mouse was
pleased. He had
never been to the
country. He packed
his bag. He went
to the country
the same day.

The country mouse
was waiting for
him.
"Please come in,"
said the country
mouse.

The country mouse showed the town mouse his house. It did not take long. His house was very small.

The country mouse liked his small house. It was cosy. The town mouse thought it a bit TOO small.

The country mouse got some food
ready. There was barleycorn and
roots. The country mouse had roots
every day. Roots and barleycorn
were the only food he had. He was
used to them. He liked them.
The town mouse did not like them
at all. He pulled a face.

The town mouse felt sorry for the country mouse. He would not like to live in a small house. He would not like to eat roots all the time. "Come to the town and stay with me," said the town mouse. "I will show you what good living is about."

The country mouse packed his bag.
He locked the door of his house.
Then he went to the town with the
town mouse.

The country mouse had never been to
the town. It was very busy.
They came to some steps.
"What a big house," said the
country mouse.
"This is where I live," said the
town mouse. "Come in."

The town mouse took the country mouse to the larder. The country mouse gasped. He had never seen so much food in one place. There was flour and oatmeal, figs and honey and dates.

"Help yourself," said the town mouse. "Can I?" said the country mouse. "Of course you can," said the town mouse. "Eat whatever you like." The country mouse liked the look of the dates. He had never seen a date before. He sniffed it. It smelt good.

The country mouse nibbled at the date. He liked the taste. Suddenly the town mouse pricked up his ears.

"Quick!" said the town mouse. "Someone is coming. We must hide." The two mice ran and hid in a tiny hole.

They waited until it was safe to come out. They seemed to wait a long time. The country mouse did not like hiding. He wanted to eat that date. At last the town mouse said it was safe to leave the hole.

The country mouse
finished the date.
He started to eat
a fig.
Suddenly the town
mouse pricked up
his ears.

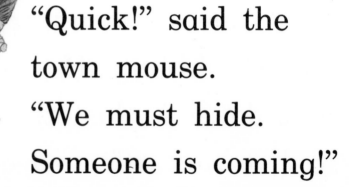

"Quick!" said the
town mouse.
"We must hide.
Someone is coming!"

The two mice hid again.
"Does this happen often?" asked the country mouse.
"Oh, all the time," said the town mouse. "You will soon get used to it."

"I do not want to get used to it," said the country mouse. "I do not like running to hide when I am eating. It makes my tummy ache. I am going home."

The country mouse was very glad to
be home. He might have only roots
to eat, but at least he could eat
them in peace.

All these appear in the pages of
the story. Can you find them?

town mouse

country mouse

letter

barleycorn

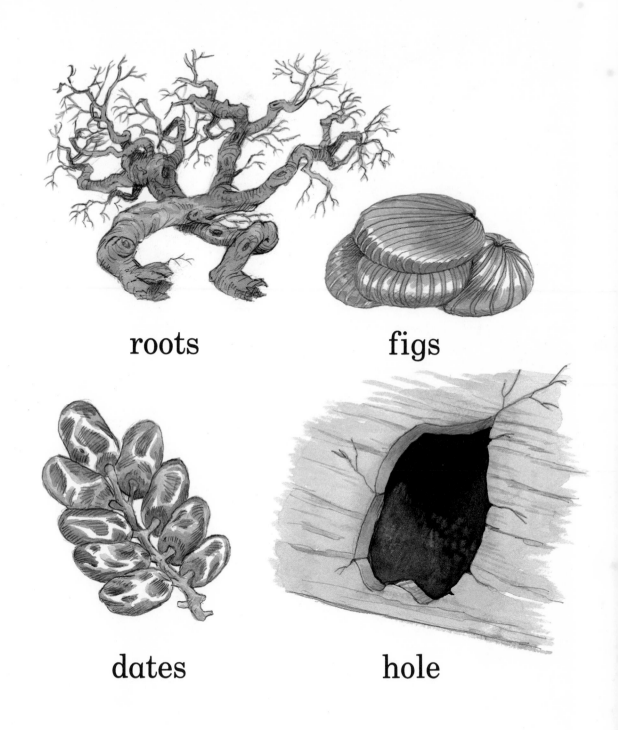

roots

figs

dates

hole

Use the pictures to tell the story
in your own words, and then draw
your own pictures.

Once there were two mice.
One mouse lived in a house in the
middle of a town. He was called
the town mouse.